I Was There...

ESCAPE FROM THE BLITZ

While every effort has been made to trace the original characters and actual historical events, some situations and people are fictional, created by the author.

Scholastic Children's Books
Euston House,
24 Eversholt Street
London, NW1 1DB, UK

A division of Scholastic Ltd
London ~ New York ~ Toronto ~ Sydney ~ Auckland
Mexico City ~ New Delhi ~ Hong Kong

First published in the UK by Scholastic Ltd, 2015

Text copyright © Tony Bradman, 2015

Illustrations by Michael Garton
© Scholastic Ltd, 2015

ISBN 978 1407 14503 7

Printed and bound by CPI Group (UK) Ltd, Croydon, CR0 4YY

1 3 5 7 9 10 8 6 4 2

I Was There...

ESCAPE FROM THE BLITZ

Tony Bradman

SCHOLASTIC

CHAPTER ONE

"I don't care what you say, I'm not going," I muttered.

Mum and Dad glanced at each other and sighed. The three of us were sitting round the table in our little kitchen – Dad in his shirtsleeves and braces, Mum in her pinny. They'd been on at me all through tea, and I was determined not to give in.

"Don't be like that, Betty," said Dad. "We're only thinking of you."

"You have to go," said Mum. "War might break out any day now."

It was the 30th of August 1939, and most grown-ups were convinced Germany was about to start a war. I wasn't so sure. Mind you, I wouldn't have been surprised if that horrible Mr Hitler did something nasty. He was the leader of the Germans. I'd seen him on the newsreels at the pictures and he usually looked dead cross. He seemed to want to take over every country in the world. First it was Austria, then somewhere called Czechoslovakia, and now for some reason he was angry with Poland.

To be honest, I hadn't been very interested in things like that before. I mean, the news on the wireless and in the paper Mum and Dad read was always bad. But I was paying attention now. It wasn't just 'the news' any more. This was about me.

"I still don't understand why that means I have to be sent away," I said. I tried to make it sound as dramatic and terrible as possible. Well, that's how I felt!

"Oh Betty, it's not like that, I promise you," said Mum, giving me a sad smile. She's small, almost tiny – petite is the word she uses – and she has a pretty face and wavy blonde hair. Dad is tall and gangly and dark, and they've always said I'm a mix of both of them – not too tall, not too skinny, and my hair is mousy brown. "Not how you mean, at any rate," she went on. "This is different. You're being evacuated."

I opened my mouth to argue, but Dad held his hand up to silence me. "I'll explain it for you once more, and then I hope you'll stop being so bloomin' stubborn."

Now it was my turn to sigh. I listened to him, but I'd heard it all before. Apparently as soon as the war started, the sky over London would be full of German planes and they would bomb us to smithereens. That's what the government said, anyway. So they'd come up with this daft plan to send us kids to the countryside. Oh, sorry, I should have said evacuated. Although I reckoned that was just one of those big fancy words grown-ups use when they want something to sound really important.

Of course I'd asked loads of questions – like, if it was going to be that bad, why weren't Mum and Dad being evacuated too, and where would I be staying, and how long would I be away? Of course Mum and Dad had all the answers. They said I'd be taken to a place in Devon with the kids and teachers from my school, and we'd live there with families who had volunteered to put us up till it was safe to come back. Our parents had to stay behind 'so they could keep everything going'.

But how exactly would they manage that? Dad was a postman – wouldn't it be a bit difficult to deliver letters in the middle of an air raid? And what would there be to come back to if the whole of Bermondsey had been blown to pieces?

It was all pretty terrifying if I really let myself think about it – being sent off to live with strangers, bombs being dropped, not knowing when I'd be coming back, Mum and Dad in danger. So it was easier to tell myself instead that the whole thing was utterly barmy, and everybody was panicking for no reason. But then that's grown-ups for you, isn't it?

Dad had finally stopped droning on. He sat there with Mum, both of them waiting for me to say I was going to be a good little girl and do as I was told, I suppose. I had another question for them, though. The most important question of all.

"Tell me this then," I said. "Who'll take care of Smoky if I'm not here?"

Smoky is our cat, and Mum and Dad don't love him like I do. He's as black as coal, not very big, and quite old – I'm nearly eleven and we've had Smoky as long as I can remember. I used to dress him up in baby clothes and wheel him around in a toy pram. Even now I sometimes pop him in a shopping basket so I can take him out with me. He doesn't complain. Mum and Dad are always moaning about him, though.

He brings us dead rats as presents, and Mum hates that, and she says I shouldn't let him sleep on my bed because he's dirty. She's wrong, though. He is a bit battered – one of his ears is bent, and he's lost the end of his tail. He's a real street cat – he spends most of his time outdoors and isn't frightened of anything. But he keeps himself clean, and he's the sweetest pussycat you could hope to meet. Mum didn't have any more kids after me, but Smoky is nicer than any brother or sister could ever be.

"Er… we will, of course," said Dad. He glanced at Mum again, and I have to say they both looked a bit shifty. Almost as if they suddenly felt uncomfortable.

"I bet you won't," I said. "I'm usually the one who remembers to feed him and fill his water bowl. If it wasn't for me you'd let him starve or die of thirst."

"Oh, Betty, that's not true," said Mum. "We wouldn't let Smoky suffer!"

She pulled her hanky from the sleeve of her dress and loudly blew her nose. For a second I thought she was about to start crying… Dad obviously thought the same, because he patted Mum's shoulder the way he does whenever she's upset. What a state they'd worked themselves into! Suddenly I needed to get out of there.

"Is it all right if I go round to Mabel's?" I said. I didn't wait for an answer.

I slammed the front door behind me as hard as I could.

CHAPTER TWO

Mabel is my best friend from school. She lives a couple of streets away in a terrace house just like mine. It has a front room for sitting in, a kitchen at the back with a little scullery, a tiny yard with an outside toilet, and a couple of small bedrooms upstairs. That's fine for Mum and Dad and me, but Mabel and her three younger sisters all have to share a bed. Mabel didn't seem to mind – I'd hate it.

I love the evenings in the school summer holidays when it stays light till really late. If the weather is good, the streets round our way can be as crowded and noisy as a school playground – there are kids everywhere. The girls skip and play tag and hopscotch, and the boys play cricket or football. Sometimes us girls join in the boys' games – we're much better than them, but the boys won't ever admit that.

Mabel's mum and dad were in the street outside their house when I arrived. Her dad was putting strips of sticky white tape over the windows while her mum looked on, arms folded. Her hair was in curlers and covered with a headscarf.

"I don't think that's right," she was saying. "Shouldn't it go on the inside?"

Mabel's dad shrugged. He worked at the docks, and was still wearing his working clothes and heavy boots. "Can't see as it'll make much difference," he said. "A silly little bit of tape ain't gonna be much help when the bombs start going off, is it?"

We'd had the government leaflet about taping our windows as well. It was supposed to stop the glass breaking into small splinters if a bomb landed outside. My Dad had already taped our windows, and as far as I could see most of the other families in

Bermondsey had done the same. But I agreed with Mabel's dad. Big splinters, small splinters – they'd all be pretty dangerous, wouldn't they?

Their front door was wide open. I yelled for Mabel and she came running out. As usual, we headed through the streets towards Southwark Park. Mabel is little and plump, has short, dark hair, and talks nineteen to the dozen. I don't mind that – I'm a talker myself – but tonight I didn't let her get started.

"So what have your mum and dad said about you being evacuated?" I asked.

Mabel shrugged just like her dad. "They ain't letting me and my sisters go," she said. "Mum says she'd rather we was all killed together than be separated."

"That's one way of looking at it, I suppose," I said. Although secretly I was a bit shocked. "It's a bit on the gloomy side, isn't it? What did your dad say?"

"He didn't like it, and they had a row," said Mabel. "But Mum said she was only being practical, so he gave in. Mum reckons a lot of people feel the same."

Just then we turned a corner and found ourselves walking past a long queue of people: men and women of all ages and a few kids. Each and every one of them had a dog on a leash, or was holding a cat, or had a birdcage with a canary or a budgie in it. There was even an old gentleman with a parrot that kept squawking loudly. The people all looked dead miserable, and some were actually crying.

"Blimey, why's the vet so busy today?" I said to Mabel. The queue stretched right along the street and into the vet's surgery. I'd made Mum and Dad take Smoky there a couple of times when he'd seemed poorly

or had been in a fight. Not often, mind, because he really hated it and Dad always grumbled about how much it cost.

"Didn't you hear?" said Mabel. "The government says everybody should have their pets put down. It's a good job we ain't got any. I wanted a rabbit but Mum…"

"What, you mean… killed?" I interrupted. I could hardly believe what I was hearing.

It seemed like the daftest thing of all. Why would they tell someone to kill their parrot?

Mabel nodded. "It was in another leaflet…" She rattled on about what the leaflet had said – pets might distract people from the war effort, whatever that was, the food you gave to your pets could be given to farm animals instead, and that was much more important, your pets couldn't be protected in air raids and might suffer…

I felt my blood freeze. I remembered the shifty expressions on Mum and Dad's faces when I'd asked who'd take care of Smoky if I wasn't around. They must have had the same leaflet as Mabel's parents – and not told me! "We wouldn't let Smoky suffer." So that was why they wanted me out of the way! Now I understood why they'd been uncomfortable – although maybe the right word was guilty.

They knew I would never agree to it, that I'd fight to keep Smoky from being killed. I was so angry. How could they even think of doing such a thing? Smoky was part of our family! I decided grown-ups weren't just daft, they were cruel and heartless. That's probably why they started all their horrible wars in the first place.

But what if I couldn't make them listen to me? What if they insisted? It was just too awful! Suddenly I had another thought, and I realized I might have the answer…

"You all right, Betty?" said Mabel at last. "You've gone dead quiet."

"What? Sorry, Mabel, I've got to go. Don't worry, I'm fine."

Smoky would be fine too. I was going to make sure of it.

CHAPTER THREE

I ran all the way home. I'd realized there was only one thing for it. I knew I wouldn't get far if I argued with Mum and Dad about Smoky. I'd just have to go along with being evacuated – and secretly take Smoky with me. I didn't have a clue yet how I was actually going to manage it, but I was sure I could think of a plan.

Smoky was sitting on our doorstep when I arrived, as if he was waiting for me. I scooped him into my arms for a cuddle and he nuzzled against my cheek.

"I love you, Smoky," I whispered into his ear – not the one that was bent, the straight

one – and he purred. "I swear I'll take care of you, whatever happens."

I went into the kitchen. Smoky jumped down and made a beeline for his food bowl, which had the scraps from our tea in it. Dad was sitting at the table reading the evening paper and Mum was doing the washing up. They both turned to look at me.

"All right, I'll do what you want," I said. "You can have me evacuated."

"Oh, Betty love!" said Mum. She burst into tears and hugged me tight.

"'Ere, get off!" I said, pushing her away. I've never been one for hugging or talking about my feelings. "I thought you'd be pleased!"

"I am, of course I am!" She pulled out her hanky and dabbed her eyes. "It's just… it's just that…" Then she got all choked and waved her hands at Dad.

"Er… I think your Mum is trying to say we'll miss you, sweetheart."

His eyes were watery too, and for a moment I thought I might start blubbing as well. Me and Mum and Dad have always been close. But then I remembered what they were planning to do to Smoky and I felt cross all over again.

"This won't do," said Mum at last, wiping

her eyes with her hanky. "We should make a start on packing your case. There's a list of the things you'll need."

"Case?" I said, my mind suddenly racing. "I didn't even know we had one."

Apparently Mum and Dad kept it under their bed. Dad fetched it down, and as soon as I saw the case I knew it would be the answer to my prayers. It was old and brown and square and a bit scuffed and dented, but Smoky would fit inside.

"Mind you, now that I'm looking at it, I wonder if it's a bit big for you…" said Mum, frowning. "I mean, you've got to be able to pick it up, haven't you?"

"You're right," said Dad. "Maybe we should find her something smaller."

"No, it's perfect!" I said quickly. "Er… can I have a look at that list?"

"Of course you can," said Mum. I breathed

a sigh of relief as she went off to fetch it from the sideboard in the front room. The list was on the other side of a letter from my school, just like the normal letters we got about the Christmas play or Sports Day. But this one gave all the details for the evacuation – the date, the time we were supposed to meet at school, the station where we'd be catching the train.

My tummy did a couple of flips as I read it — we would be leaving on Friday the 1st of September. That was two days from now!

Mum went over the list. It wasn't long. "Toothbrush and toothpaste, flannel and soap, spare clothes, underwear, socks, your nightdress, a proper coat — yours is too big to go in the case so you'll have to wear it. A packed lunch for the journey…"

That night, Mum and Dad left the case on the floor beside my bed. I turned my bedside light off at the usual time, but I didn't go to sleep, not even when Mum and Dad came upstairs and went to bed themselves. I had a lot to think about. My mind was in a whirl — I was scared about going away and about what was going to happen to me and Mum and Dad, and Smoky, of course. I was determined to save him — but the more I thought about it, the more I realized it might not be easy…

I wasn't too worried about getting Smoky into the case. He always did what I wanted him to, and it would be a bit like when I took him shopping. As soon as he turned up on Friday, I'd pop him in the case and shut it. He stayed out at night during the summer, then climbed the drainpipe at the back of the house early in the morning to get into my room. I always left my window open for him.

No, the problem might be keeping him in the case. The letter from school didn't say how long it would take to get to Devon, but I had a feeling it was going to be quite a long journey. I made two little holes in the case so Smoky would be able to breathe – I hoped Mum and Dad wouldn't notice. I was also hoping Smoky wouldn't need to go to the toilet on the way there. That could be a disaster.

And what about when we got to Devon? What would I do with Smoky once we were there? I could feel myself getting more and more worked up. How could I possibly pull off something like this? It was mad even to think about it! But then I calmed down. I realized I had no idea what it would be like in the country, so I decided not to worry about it till I had to.

I tried again to go to sleep, but I couldn't. I tossed and turned, and after a while I quietly got out of bed and went over to the window. There's not much of a view from my room, only our little yard and the backs of the houses in the next street. But there was a full moon, and everything was bathed in a strange silver light.

Suddenly the world outside looked very strange and scary. I didn't really want to be evacuated. I wanted to stay at home with

Mum and Dad. But then I remembered to be cross with them because of what I knew they were planning to do.

If I didn't get Smoky out of London, he was doomed.

CHAPTER FOUR

As usual the next day, Dad left the house to go to work long before I was awake. Mum was up early too so she could make sure the clothes I was taking were washed and dried and ironed, ready to be packed. Not that I've got a lot – one dress for school, one to wear outside school, a couple of jumpers, some vests, pants and socks, one nightdress. I'd be wearing my school shoes – I didn't have any others.

All that kept Mum busy and out of the way for most of the morning, which was good. It meant I could secretly give Smoky some practice in the case. As I'd guessed, he didn't need much persuading. He sniffed at it for a while, but then he climbed inside and curled up for a snooze. I gently closed the lid and counted to one hundred… and when I opened it, he was still fast asleep and purring.

Of course, I soon hit a snag. When Mum packed my case later that evening it was pretty full. I realized I'd have to take stuff out of it to make room for Smoky. Fine, I thought – I could live without most of the vests and pants and socks. But I wouldn't be able to do it till after Mum and Dad had gone to bed, and then I'd have to find a hiding place for what I took out. I decided I'd stuff it all under my mattress.

There was another problem, too. For the first time ever, it seemed Mum and Dad didn't want me to go to bed. And when I did, they kept coming up to see me.

"All right, love?" Mum would say. "Need anything, sweetheart?" said Dad.

They were both weepy and sad-looking, and that nearly set me off once or twice. In the end I had to pretend I was asleep. I wasn't, though. I spent half the night wide awake, terrified Smoky wouldn't turn up early enough in the morning. But he did, and everything went smoothly – undies and socks out and hidden, Smoky in and fast asleep.

Then disaster struck. Dad suddenly appeared in my bedroom doorway.

"Thought you might need a hand with your case, sweetheart," he said, striding over and picking it up. It was a good job I'd managed to get it shut before he'd come in. "Blimey, what have you got in here? The bloomin' thing must weigh a ton!"

"What? Nothing!" I squeaked and tried to grab it. "I can carry it!"

But Dad had already set off down the stairs, the case swinging in his hand. I'd planned to be careful with it, and I had a sudden vision of poor Smoky being wildly thrown about inside. I winced, expecting to hear him start howling at any second. By some miracle he didn't. Dad dumped the case by the front door and not a peep came out of it.

Mum insisted on cooking me an enormous breakfast – bacon, eggs, fried bread – and she and Dad sat there watching me eat every mouthful. "Come on, we're supposed to be at school by nine," Dad said at last. "We mustn't be late."

I was wearing my school dress and shoes and my school cardigan. Mum helped me into my coat. I scowled when I saw a label tied to one of the buttons with a bit of string. My name – 'Elizabeth Joan Grimwade' – and my date of birth were written on one side, and the name and address of my school on the other. Elizabeth is my proper name, but it always looks really peculiar to me when I see it written down – everyone calls me Betty. But that wasn't the only reason I didn't like the label.

"I don't really have to wear this, do I?" I said. "It makes me feel like a parcel."

"Sorry, love," said Mum, smiling. "There's no getting out of it, I'm afraid."

"You're not like the parcels we see down at the sorting office," said Dad. "They don't talk back and give us loads of cheek. Right, I'll carry your case..."

My school is a ten-minute walk away, and I didn't take my eyes off that case till we arrived. But then I looked around, surprised. Three double-decker buses were parked by the school gates, and a crowd of parents and children stood beside them. I reckoned about half the school was there, mostly the older kids. There were little ones as well, holding on to their parents or their big brothers or sisters. Most of the grown-ups were pretending to be cheerful, but some of the mums were crying.

I heard some of the parents asking our headmaster, Mr Jenner, how long the evacuation was likely to last, and he said he had no idea. "That depends on the government," he said. "And the Germans, of course." I could tell that was probably the wrong thing to say. The mums who seemed the most upset just cried louder.

All the kids had cases and labels on their coats like me, and carried their gas masks too. That was something else the government said we had to do, in case the Germans attacked us with poison gas. The masks were horrible rubbery things that came in a cardboard box with a string attached so you could carry it over your shoulder.

I could see Mr Jenner in the crowd – he's tall and has white hair. He was doing a lot of shouting, and I have to say things seemed slightly out of control. I spotted several other teachers behind him, including Miss Harrison, my teacher from last year. She's young, dark-haired and pretty, and really nice. She saw Mum and Dad and me and came over to us, pushing through the crowd.

Everything happened quickly after that. "Lovely to see you, Betty!" she said, smiling. "You're in Bus A with me!"

Somebody grabbed my case and put it upstairs on the bus with all the other cases, and the teachers started to hustle us on too. Mum hugged and kissed me and so did Dad, and Mum said something I didn't catch. Then I was on the bus looking out of the window as it drove off.

Mum and Dad waved, and I felt tears running down my cheeks. I waved back at them, but soon the bus went round the corner and I couldn't see them any more.

Smoky and I were on our way to Devon.

CHAPTER FIVE

We were going to Paddington train station first, and the journey across London in the bus was very strange. It was a bit like being on a school outing, and some of the kids were laughing and singing. A lot weren't though, especially the little ones. Most were sitting in their seats looking worried, and quite a few were sobbing. Mr Jenner and Miss Harrison were on our bus, and Miss Harrison spent a lot of time trying to calm them.

But the strangest thing for me was the view through the bus windows. Bermondsey is just over the river from the centre of London, and Mum and Dad had often taken me to 'see the sights' like St Paul's Cathedral or the Tower of London, or to head 'up west', to look at the posh shops on Oxford Street.

It all looked different now. Our buses went over Westminster Bridge, so we got a glimpse of the Houses of Parliament. There were sandbags stacked up round the gates and soldiers on patrol behind them. The entrances of other buildings we passed also had sandbags round their doors, and in some of the squares and parks gangs of workmen were busily digging big holes – for air-raid shelters, I realized.

There were always soldiers at Buckingham Palace, to protect the King and Queen and their daughters, Elizabeth and Margaret. But they'd swapped their red jackets for brown ones, and those funny furry hats they wear for tin helmets. Then in Hyde Park we saw even more soldiers. They were winching a

giant balloon up into the sky. It was bigger than our bus, a great silver thing like some gigantic toy. I asked Miss Harrison what it was, and she said it was a 'barrage' balloon. They were supposed to make it difficult for German planes to fly low over London.

I was beginning to wonder if there might actually be something in what the grown-ups were saying about a war. They certainly seemed to be taking the idea pretty seriously… But then I suddenly realized I hadn't given poor Smoky a single thought since we'd got on the bus, and I felt terrible. What if the holes I'd made in the case weren't enough? What if Smoky was gasping for breath at that very second?

"Are you all right, Betty?" said Miss Harrison. "You've gone awfully pale."

She was standing next to where I was sitting, a concerned look on her face. "I'm fine, Miss," I said. "Er… I didn't sleep very well last night, that's all."

"I'm not surprised," Miss Harrison said, squeezing my shoulder. "It's hard to be separated from your parents. But don't worry, we'll take care of you."

Of course, I smiled like a good little girl. I couldn't tell her the truth: that I hadn't been lying awake worrying about being separated from Mum and Dad. I had to keep Smoky secret from her and Mr Jenner too. So I sat there, staring at the ceiling above my head with my fingers crossed, hoping Smoky was all right.

Moments later, we arrived at Paddington. The buses stopped in the street and I jumped straight out of my seat. "Can I get my case, sir?" I asked Mr Jenner.

"No, you can't," he snapped. "I'll find a couple of porters to put our bags in the train's luggage compartment. Get the children organized, Miss Harrison."

That was easier said than done. We tumbled off the buses, but dozens of other buses were already there and more were arriving all the time, each bringing kids and teachers from every part of London. Miss Harrison had to shout a lot to make sure we stayed together and didn't get mixed up with any other schools. Mr Jenner was gone a while, but he came back at last, bringing a couple of porters pulling big trollies.

They immediately started chucking our cases onto them. I could hardly bear to look, but luckily, soon I didn't have to. Mr Jenner marched us off to our train.

There was more chaos inside the station. The platforms were packed with kids and teachers yelling at them, or at each other. Nobody seemed to know which trains to get on, and it took ages to find ours. But we did in the end, and Mr Jenner and Miss Harrison herded us into the right carriage. I managed to grab a window seat, and I was relieved to see our cases being loaded into a carriage further down. Eventually the train pulled out and we began to leave good old London behind. I almost started blubbing again – and quite a few of my schoolmates did start crying.

I have to say that what followed was one of the worst days of my life. The journey lasted for hours, and I was worried sick about Smoky the whole way.

I desperately wanted to go and check on him, so I asked Miss Harrison if I could fetch something from my case. But that wasn't allowed. I thought about sneaking off when I went to the toilet – there was one at the end of the carriage. But Mr Jenner and Miss Harrison watched us like hawks, and I knew I'd never get away with it.

In the end I just sat staring out of the window, watching towns and villages and fields crawl past. Miss Harrison made everyone sing songs like 'Wish Me Luck As You Wave Me Goodbye' and 'Doing the Lambeth Walk'. My schoolmates seemed more cheerful now, even the little ones, almost as if this was only an outing.

I didn't want to sing. I couldn't be happy till I knew Smoky was all right. I didn't talk to any of my schoolmates, not even when they tried to talk to me.

"Cheer up, Betty," said Miss Harrison. "You mustn't be downhearted."

I looked at her. But I didn't say a word.

CHAPTER SIX

We didn't get to where we were supposed to be till the early evening. The train kept stopping and starting again, and at one point Mr Jenner had a blazing row with the driver. So, as you can imagine, nobody was singing by the time we arrived, not even Miss Harrison. We'd eaten our packed lunches ages ago, and we were all starving. Everybody was tired and fed up, and most of the little ones were snivelling.

The tiny station we finally stopped at was in the middle of nowhere. We tumbled out of the carriages and stood on the platform, a hundred kids huddled behind our teachers.

Some people were waiting for us – a vicar with a bald head and glasses, a couple of snooty-looking women in posh clothes, and an elderly man holding a clipboard. He was frowning, and the other three didn't seem too happy either.

Mr Jenner strode up to him, and they shook hands. But they were soon arguing.

"I'm sorry, we simply weren't expecting so many," said the man, glancing at his clipboard. "We were told we'd have to find homes for no more than twenty."

"That's utterly ridiculous!" said Mr Jenner, his face red. "What do you expect us to do now? We can't just turn round and take them back to London, can we?"

Miss Harrison and the other teachers were looking worried, and my heart sank. I couldn't face the idea of getting on the train again. Judging by the moans and groans of the kids around me, nobody else could either. But then we were saved.

"All right, all right!" said the man with the clipboard at last, raising his voice. "We'll have to make do somehow. You'd better come to the village hall."

It turned out there were no buses, so we had to walk, and carry our own cases. The train driver and our teachers were handing them out, and I barged through to the front of the queue. I grabbed my case and hurried further along the platform, away from everybody else. I put it down and knelt beside it as if I was checking my shoe buckle. I didn't dare open it. I couldn't let Smoky out − if he was even still alive.

"Smoky! Can you hear me?" I whispered. Silence. I said it again, and heard a faint "Miaow!" I was so relieved I hugged the case and almost started blubbing. He sounded a bit cross, but I couldn't blame him for that. I'd be cheesed off if I'd been stuck in a case for as long as he had. But at least he wasn't dead! "You'll have to be quiet now, Smoky," I said. "I'll get you out soon, I promise…"

I picked up the case – Dad had been right, it was heavy – and joined the others. We trudged out of the station in a straggly column behind Mr Jenner, who was following the man with the clipboard. It was getting dark, so I couldn't see much of the village. Not that there was much to see – just a street with a butcher's, a greengrocer, a pub and a church with a small hall behind it, which is where we were heading.

There were more people inside the hall, some ladies behind a table loaded with plates of sandwiches and cakes and jugs of orange squash and lemonade. A crowd of kids made a dash for it, pushing and shoving each other out of the way to stuff sandwiches in their mouths and get a drink. "Children, please!" yelled Mr Jenner. "Remember your manners…" But it was too late. Soon everything had vanished.

The ladies behind the table looked horrified, and tut-tutted and muttered among themselves. The original group from the station were doing the same, but by that point I couldn't have cared less. I felt so tired I didn't know how I was still standing up. Everybody else had put their cases down, but I held on to mine. I wasn't going to be parted from it ever again, not if I could help it.

The next half an hour was a bit of a blur. The grown-ups did a lot of arguing, and more arrived to join in. Miss Harrison explained to us what was happening. Some families who had volunteered to take in one child now said they'd have two, even three. Families from other villages had been asked if they'd help out, and the hall gradually began to empty. Eventually only about a dozen of us kids were left.

By then I could barely keep my eyes open. I remember standing in a line while a couple of even more snooty-looking women walked along, staring at us. "They seem rather… common," one whispered to her pal. "Are you sure they're clean?"

That woke me up a bit. It wasn't a nice thing to say, and I nearly told her so. But I didn't. I was glad to see Miss Harrison giving the woman a look, though.

Then another posh lady arrived. She was wearing a nice skirt, a jacket with a fur collar, and a hat with a narrow brim – I think it's called a Trilby. I could tell the grown-ups thought she was important. They were practically tripping over themselves to help her.

"Lady Musgrave, so good of you to come!" said the man with the clipboard. "We hardly expected someone of your standing to get involved in this…"

"Nonsense, we must all do our bit," she said, like she was telling him off.

Blimey, I thought. She was so posh it probably cost five bob just to talk to her. Someone like that wouldn't want a Betty from Bermondsey staying with her, would she now? But Miss Harrison pointed at me, and her Ladyship came over.

"How do you do, Betty?" she said. "Would you like to come with me?"

I picked up my case and followed her into the dark night. I don't think I've ever felt quite so nervous. I had no idea what was lying in store for me…

CHAPTER SEVEN

At least I wouldn't have to walk this time
– there was a car waiting outside the hall.
I'd never been in one before – ordinary
people couldn't afford to have cars, only
posh people with lots of money. The car
certainly looked very impressive, even in the
dark. The driver jumped out and held the
back door open for Lady Musgrave. He was
short and stocky and almost as old as Mr
Jenner, with grey hair and a grumpy face.

"This is Betty, Arthur," said Lady Musgrave.
"You can take us home now."

"Right you are, your Ladyship," Arthur
growled. He had a proper country accent,

like a farmer in a film. He frowned and reached for my case, and I couldn't bring myself to let it go. We had a brief tussle, but he won and slung it in the boot.

I winced inside – poor Smoky! – but there was nothing I could do about it. So I sat in the back seat of the car with Lady Musgrave, and Arthur got in and drove us out of the village. It was warm and cosy in the car, and the seat was soft and deep and very comfortable. Soon I felt more tired than ever, and couldn't stop yawning.

"Poor you!" murmured Lady Musgrave. "Has it been a terribly long day?"

"Not half," I said. I felt peculiar, almost as if I was dreaming. The car's lights lit up the road ahead, but there was nothing on either side of us except blackness.

"Well, you'll soon be able to relax," said Lady Musgrave. "It's not far now."

A few moments later we slowed down and turned off the road. We went up a long drive lined with trees that loomed out of the dark, and stopped at last in front of a big house. We all got out of the car and Arthur went round the back to take my case from the boot. Then he stomped off with it towards the house. He pushed open the front door and disappeared inside. Lady Musgrave and I followed him.

It's hard to describe exactly how I felt at that moment. I'd never been in a house like that, so I suppose I was stunned. The hallway was enormous, probably about the size of my entire house, with several doors on both sides. There was a huge flight of stairs in the middle, like something from a palace in a Hollywood movie.

"Hilda, we're back!" Lady Musgrave called out. "Is supper ready?"

One of the doors opened and a woman came out. She was short and round, with frizzy dark hair trapped in a bun. Her cheeks were rosy, and she was wearing a pinny a couple of sizes too small. "It is," she said. "But it's only sandwiches, mind."

"I'm sure that will do splendidly!" said Lady Musgrave. "And is our guest's room ready too? I have a feeling she'll want to go to bed as soon as she's eaten."

"Oh yes, your Ladyship," said Hilda. "All done, sheets changed…"

"Jolly good," said Lady Musgrave. "Well, Betty, this way to the kitchen."

"What about my case?" I said. Arthur was still standing there with it.

"Don't worry," said Lady Musgrave. "Arthur will take it up for you."

I wanted to argue, but I was so tired and there didn't seem much point. Besides, the idea of eating something had made my mouth water and my tummy rumble. So I followed Lady Musgrave, although I watched my case till I couldn't see it any more.

The kitchen was enormous too. There was a giant black iron cooker, loads of pots and pans hanging up, and a table you could have got my whole class round. A plate of cheese sandwiches was waiting for me, neatly cut although the bread was thick.

"Would you like something to drink?" said Lady Musgrave. She sat beside me at the table while Hilda hovered in the background. "Squash? Some milk, perhaps?"

"If it's all the same to you, I'd rather have a cup of tea," I said, biting into a sandwich. Lady Musgrave raised an eyebrow and Hilda gave me a bit of a look. But the tea she made me was hot and strong and sweet, just the way I like it.

"I expect you want to know a bit more about us," said Lady Musgrave. "And I'd certainly like to find out about you. But we can leave all that for tomorrow."

Once I'd finished eating, Lady Musgrave took me upstairs. My room was at the end of a long corridor, and it was amazing. There was a huge bed with loads of pillows, a chest of drawers and a wardrobe, and shelves full of books and teddy bears. A door led to a small bathroom with its own toilet. I couldn't believe it – an indoor toilet! There was a bath and a sink too, and shelves full of little bottles and soaps.

But the most important thing was my case. And there it was, standing on the floor at the end of the bed. It was all I could do not to open it straightaway.

"This is my daughter's room," said Lady Musgrave. She opened the window and a cool breeze wafted in. "Or at least it used to be. She's grown up now and has her own family… So, will you be all right?" I looked round at her and nodded, and she smiled. "Well, I'll leave you to it then. Good night, Betty. I hope you'll be happy with us. I'll see you in the morning. But don't worry, you can sleep as late as you like."

Then she was gone, the door softly clicking shut after her. I instantly leapt on my case and opened it. Smoky was all tangled in my clothes, and for a terrifying second I thought he wasn't breathing. Then he looked at me and I knew he was fine.

I picked him up and lay down on the bed to give him a proper cuddle. "I'm sorry, Smoky, but we're here now and you're safe," I whispered as he nuzzled against me and purred. The bed was very comfortable and I closed my eyes, just for a second, I thought…

When I woke up early the next morning Smoky was gone.

CHAPTER EIGHT

I'd been having a nightmare about Mr Hitler and Mum and Dad. Mr Hitler was holding a bomb like the ones in the funny films, a round black thing with a fizzing fuse. Mum and Dad were in our house, hiding under the kitchen table with their hands over their ears. Mr Hitler laughed and chucked the bomb through a taped-up window, there was an enormous BANG! – and suddenly I was wide awake.

I sat bolt upright in bed, my heart thumping. I was still in the nightmare, terrified that Mum and Dad were dead. I heard a strange sound coming from somewhere outside –

COCK-A-DOODLE DOO! – and the nightmare faded away. Suddenly everything came flooding back. Leaving home, the train journey, Lady Musgrave, being driven to her house, letting Smoky out of my case...

Smoky! Where was he? The last thing I remembered was cuddling him as I fell asleep, but now he was nowhere to be seen. He wasn't on the bed, or in it, or under it, or in the case, or in the bathroom. I began to panic, my heart started thumping again, and terrible thoughts filled my mind. What if Lady Musgrave had come back into the room after I'd fallen asleep and seen him? What if she had taken Smoky away?

Then I remembered the open window, and I knew where Smoky had gone.

I rushed over to it and looked out. I'd only seen the front of the house the night before, and that had been in the dark. Now it was the morning, and I saw that Lady Musgrave's house didn't have a back yard like my house in London, it had a back garden almost the size of Southwark Park! Most of it was grass, but there were lots of big bushes down both sides, and a whole forest at the far end. The sun was only just starting to peek over the trees, so I realized it must be very early. I wondered where that cock-a-doodle-doo had come from – maybe there was a farm somewhere nearby.

I could see drainpipes below the window, and a small tree with branches close to the wall. So it would have been easy for Smoky to climb down. But where was he now? I scanned the garden – and there he was, doing a wee by a bush! When he'd finished he looked up at me, bold as brass. Then he sauntered off like he didn't have a care in the world, and slipped into the shadows beneath another bush.

Well, I was in a proper state at that moment, and no mistake. I was cross with Smoky for running off, terrified Lady Musgrave might see him, and trying to work out what to do, all at the same time. Should I run down and grab him before he ran off even further? If he got lost I'd need help to find him, so maybe I should simply confess everything to Lady Musgrave...

Then I thought – hang on a minute, what am I worrying about? Lady Musgrave was probably still in bed, nobody else was in the garden, and Smoky seemed happy. He must have needed some fresh air after being cooped up in that case. So perhaps I could relax. I didn't have to worry about where he could go to the toilet, and he didn't seem bothered about being fed – I would find him something later.

Looking at him, I had a feeling he'd come back when he was good and ready. He could climb up the drainpipes like at home – I'd hide him somewhere when he did. But that could wait… I yawned, and realized how tired I'd been the night before – I was still in the clothes I'd worn on the journey. I quickly pulled them off, dug my nightdress out of my case and put it on. I climbed into bed, and soon I was asleep again.

I didn't have any more nightmares, thank goodness, and when I woke up once more I guessed it was late. I had a wash in that amazing little bathroom – I was sure even the King's daughters didn't have one as good. Then I got dressed and headed downstairs, hoping for some breakfast. There was nobody in the kitchen, but I could hear voices, and I tracked them down to a room across the hallway.

Lady Musgrave was in there with Hilda and Arthur. It was a big room full of settees and armchairs and tables, but they were all standing at one end, round a huge wireless. It was about ten times the size of the one we had at home, more like a piece of furniture than a radio – all polished brown wood and loads of winking lights.

"Ah, Betty!" said Lady Musgrave, smiling. "Did you sleep well?"

"Ssshh, he's about to speak!" Arthur hissed suddenly, then realized who he was talking to. "Oh, sorry your Ladyship, I, er... didn't mean to be rude, but..."

"Don't worry, Arthur," said Lady Musgrave. "You're quite right, we should all listen to what the Prime Minister has to say. Come and stand by me, Betty."

A man started speaking, and I recognized his voice. It was Mr Chamberlain, our Prime Minister, and he always sounded dead gloomy. 'This morning the British Ambassador in Berlin handed the German government a final note...' Apparently Mr Hitler had attacked Poland, and we'd told him to stop or else. But he wasn't taking any notice, so now Mr Chamberlain said we were 'at war with Germany.'

He could have stopped there, but he droned on for a while longer. Arthur looked grim, Hilda started crying, and Lady Musgrave put her arm round my shoulders. Then as soon as Mr Chamberlain finished, I heard a strange noise in the distance.

It was the siren to warn us that the German bombers were coming.

CHAPTER NINE

I knew what it was because I'd heard it before. They'd tested the sirens in London more than once over the last year. Mum always said they were like banshees wailing, but I had no idea what a banshee was. To begin with I thought they sounded scary, then after a while I got used to them and they stopped bothering me. But I wasn't expecting to hear a siren in the country, and suddenly I felt quite nervous.

"Quick, they're coming!" said Hilda, her face white. "Down to the cellar!"

"Don't be daft, woman!" snapped Arthur. "I reckon that's the Barnstaple siren, so it's miles away. I'll bet it's just another test, or someone trying to scare us all."

"They've certainly managed that," said Lady Musgrave. "I'm sure Arthur is right, Hilda. Why don't you make Betty something to eat? She must be starving."

My tummy rumbled as if it agreed with her, but I wasn't really bothered about eating. I kept thinking about Mum and Dad and the nightmare I'd had. Maybe they were being bombed at that very moment... To be honest, I couldn't imagine why Mr Hitler would want to bomb somewhere like Devon. There didn't seem to be much here. But London was different – that's where most of the important stuff was.

I'll admit I even began to feel guilty about the way I'd treated Mum and Dad, and worried about them, too. We were at war, just as they'd said we would be. But as

I sat there in the big kitchen, wolfing down the delicious ham sandwich Hilda made me, I decided I wasn't going to forgive them just yet. They'd been planning to have Smoky put down, for heaven's sake! If it hadn't been for me, he'd have been dead by now.

Besides, we listened to the news again a little while later, and there was nothing about any air raids on London. Of course I was pleased that Mum and Dad would be all right, but I did feel a bit cross too. The bombing had been supposed to start as soon as war was declared, or at least that's what the government had said. Well, that didn't seem to have happened – the grown-ups obviously didn't have a clue.

"So, tell me about yourself, Betty," said Lady Musgrave. "I didn't really have much chance to speak to your teacher last night. It all seemed rather chaotic."

Lady Musgrave had sent Hilda to start getting 'lunch' ready – I wondered if that was what we called 'dinner' at home. Arthur had gone off to sort out the blackout curtains for the rooms that didn't have them already. We'd had a leaflet about them too. Every house was supposed to have curtains that didn't let out any light at night. That way the Germans wouldn't be able to see where to drop their bombs.

"There's not much to tell, er… Miss." I suddenly felt shy with her. I could see now that she was old, but still good-looking, with lots of auburn hair and green eyes.

"You don't have to call me Miss," she said, smiling. "Although I'm not sure what you should call me. I suppose I'm standing in for your parents, but it wouldn't be right for you to call me Mother. How about Florence? It is my name, after all."

We talked for quite a while, and I'll say this for her – she was good at getting information out of me. I told her about my school, and Mr Jenner and Miss Harrison and my friend Mabel. I told her about Mum and Dad and living in Bermondsey. I didn't tell her we had a cat, though. I thought it best not to mention Smoky, in case she asked any awkward questions or I slipped up and gave the game away.

"Would you like to write to your parents?" she said at last. "I'm sure your teachers will let them know you've arrived safely, but they'll want to hear from you."

"No, I don't think so." She gave me a strange look, but I just shrugged.

What would I say in a letter? It would be very short. '*Dear Mum and Dad, I've secretly smuggled Smoky to the country, so you won't be able to have him put down now. Hope you're well and there aren't too many bombs. Love, Betty.*'

"Oh well, as you wish," said Lady Musgrave. "Is there anything you'd like to know about me? I thought I might give you a tour of the house and garden…"

"There is, as it happens. Who are all the people in those photographs?"

I'd noticed there were loads of framed photographs on the tables in the room – wedding pictures, men in uniforms, children.

"Those are pictures of the family," she said. "This is my daughter Daphne – you're sleeping in her old room. She's married and has two boys of her own now. They live in Scotland, so I don't see them often. And this is my son Nigel. He's in the Army, the same regiment as his father."

"That must be nice," I said. "For them to be working together, I mean."

She gave me a sad smile, just like one of Mum's. "I'm afraid my husband was killed in the last war, Betty. Wars seem to come round rather too often."

"I'm sorry," I said. I felt embarrassed. "I shouldn't have been so nosy."

"Don't be silly! I said you could ask me. I've been a widow for a long time, so I'm used to talking about it. I only wish I didn't feel quite so useless. I have plenty to keep me occupied with the house and garden, but it would be lovely to feel needed. That's why I volunteered to have you. At least I'm doing something to help."

I looked at the family photographs again. They reminded me of the pictures of the family we had at home, of me with Mum and Dad, and I almost started blubbing. But Lady Musgrave kept talking, and I blew my nose instead.

CHAPTER TEN

The tour of the house and garden was an eye-opener, to say the least. I hadn't realized how big the place was. I lost count of how many rooms there were, all stuffed with fancy furniture and rugs, and the walls were covered in old pictures. Some of the rooms didn't look as if they were used much, though.

The garden was bigger than I'd thought as well – I'd only seen part of it from my window. A path through the trees led to what Lady Musgrave called 'Arthur's Kingdom', a space the size of our school playground in London. Rows of plants filled most of it, although there was a shed in one corner, and some kind of large cage in another. Arthur was standing beside it, a worried expression on his face.

It turned out that Arthur and Hilda were married, and had a room at the top of the house. Arthur was Lady Musgrave's gardener and handyman as well as her driver. He grew a lot of vegetables, and kept chickens too – now I knew where the cock-a-doodle-doo had come from. Once I was closer to the 'cage' I could see it was a sort of little hut surrounded by wire with a lot of chickens cooped up in it. So I wasn't surprised when Lady Musgrave said it was called a chicken coop.

"Are you all right, Arthur?" she said. "Has something happened?"

"It bloomin' well has, your Ladyship," growled Arthur. "We lost a couple of chicks last night. I reckon a fox probably dug under the wire and nabbed 'em."

I saw the chicks now, little cheeping bundles of yellow bobbling about. There was a hole in the ground beneath the wire. A single yellow feather hung from it.

"I'm sorry to hear that," said Lady Musgrave. "Is there anything I can do?"

"Oh no, don't concern yourself, your Ladyship," said Arthur. "I'll fix the wire, and if the blasted creature comes back I'll soon deal with it, you see if I don't."

He nodded in the direction of something leaning against the wire – a long gun with two barrels. Dad loves cowboy films, and he'd taken me to quite a few. Cowboys always have guns, so I knew what they looked like. Still, seeing a real one was a bit of a shock. It gave me a funny feeling to think it could kill an animal or a person.

"Yes, well, I'm sure you will," said Lady Musgrave. "Come along, Betty."

We went back through the garden to the house, Lady Musgrave chatting away. But I wasn't listening. Suddenly I was worried about Smoky. I didn't like the idea of him being in this garden any more, not when there were things like foxes around – foxes that snatched chicks in the night. Not that I knew much about foxes. I'd only ever seen pictures of them in story books at school, so I knew they had red fur and big tails, but that was it. The question was – would Smoky be in danger from one?

"Excuse me, er... Florence," I said, interrupting her. I wasn't used to calling grown-ups by their first names. Especially not posh grown-ups. "How big is a fox?"

"They're quite small, like a medium-sized dog, usually," she said, smiling at me. "They're certainly no danger to people. You're not worried, are you?"

"No, not really," I said. "So why does Arthur want to shoot it, then?"

"To protect his chickens, of course. I suppose it's hard for you to understand, being from the city. But that's how it is out here in the country, Betty. Now, I wonder what Hilda has made us for lunch today?"

I did feel a bit relieved to hear foxes weren't the size of lions or tigers. I knew Smoky could take care of himself. In fact, he had a reputation round our way for being a bruiser. He was always sweet to me, but he'd never lost a fight with another cat, and he'd seen off plenty of dogs, including some big ones. It still nagged at me, though. I couldn't help thinking of those little chicks being snatched...

Lunch helped to put it out of my mind for a while. Lady Musgrave and I ate in the posh dining room, and Hilda had gone to town with the food, as Dad would have said. She'd done roast beef and potatoes and Yorkshire puddings, with apple crumble and custard for afters. I ate so much I thought my tummy was going to explode. The only time I could remember feeling that full was at Christmas.

"Nice to see someone who appreciates good cooking," said Hilda. "You make the most of it too, girl. They'll start rationing food soon, like in the last war, you mark my words." Mum had already talked about rationing. It was another one of those government things – they were probably going to limit the amount of food for everyone so the country would have enough to get through the war.

"Well, let's cross that bridge when we come to it," said Lady Musgrave. "Now, I wonder if there's anything on the wireless for you to listen to, Betty…"

But there wasn't – it was all government announcements and news bulletins. The government wanted everyone to keep calm, but that wasn't likely to happen, was it? So far the only grown-up I'd met who wasn't panicking in one way or another was Lady Musgrave. But even she looked upset when we listened to one news report. The Germans were bombing cities in Poland and lots of people were being killed.

"How terrible," Lady Musgrave said quietly, turning off the wireless.

But it was too late. All I could think of was bombs falling on a city.

And in my mind that city was London.

CHAPTER ELEVEN

I felt better later. At six o'clock we had tea, although Lady Musgrave called it 'supper'. There were sandwiches and a cake that Hilda had baked, and somehow I found a bit more room in my tummy. We didn't listen to the wireless, thank goodness. Lady Musgrave and I sat and talked about all sorts of things, but not the war. Then at about eight o'clock I said I was tired and that I wanted to go upstairs to bed.

Of course what I really wanted was to find out if Smoky was all right. I'd left the window in my room open, so I hoped he might be waiting for me. I'd even sneaked some beef and cake up for him, and I'd realized there was plenty of water in the tap for him too. But he wasn't there, and when I looked out into the garden I couldn't see him anywhere. It was starting to get dark, and the shadows of the trees and bushes were creeping across the grass. The garden seemed like a pretty scary place.

"Come on, Smoky, where are you?" I whispered. I didn't dare call him any louder, but somehow I thought he might hear me. The minutes ticked past, and he didn't appear, so after a while I decided to give up looking. As Mum always said, a watched pot never boils. I had to keep myself occupied, though, so I took a book from the shelves and lay down on the bed to have a read.

I like books. Reading was one of the best things we did at school, and Miss Harrison often let me take a book home. I'd seen this one before, too. It was called *The Railway Children*, and Miss Harrison had read us some of it last year. But I couldn't keep my mind on it. I was worried about Smoky – I'd been wondering if foxes might actually be tougher than cats and dogs, even London ones.

I was worried about Mum and Dad as well. Hearing that all those Polish cities had been badly bombed had rattled me. If the Germans could do it to Poland, then they could probably do it to Bermondsey too. I was still a bit cross with Mum and Dad, but it was getting harder to keep it up. What if I'd been wrong? What if they'd decided not to go along with what the government had said about pets?

Just then, Smoky appeared at the window with a loud MIAOW! and I nearly jumped out of my skin. "Shush!" I hissed, grabbing him. "Where have you been?"

I put him on the end of my bed and he started licking his paws. He stopped from time to time to stare at me, and I have to say he looked relaxed. He obviously hadn't been scared by anything in the garden, so I thought I could relax too.

I left the window open that night so he could get out when he wanted to, and when I woke up in the morning he was gone again. The sun was shining, but Lady Musgrave and Hilda were gloomy at breakfast. I knew they'd been listening to the wireless – I could hear the announcer's posh voice droning away as I'd come down the stairs. Lady Musgrave turned it off as soon as I went into the dining room.

Breakfast was as good as lunch the day before. There were all sorts of things in silver dishes on the sideboard – bacon, sausages, scrambled eggs, tomatoes, smoked fish with rice – I think it was called kedgeree. Hilda kept giving me seconds.

I was still eating when there was a knock on the front door. It was Miss Harrison! She'd borrowed a bike from someone in the village and come out to see me. Lady Musgrave asked her to sit at the dining table and Hilda made her a cup of tea.

"I'm sorry I couldn't manage to get here yesterday, Betty," said Miss Harrison. "But I thought you'd be all right, and there was just so much we had to do."

Apparently a lot of my schoolmates were unhappy or homesick or had been badly behaved, at least according to the families they were staying with. Poor Mr Jenner and Miss Harrison had spent most of the day going round sorting things out.

"But I do have some good news," said Miss Harrison. "The vicar has very kindly allowed us to use the church hall for teaching, and we plan to start tomorrow. We won't be able to fit everyone in at once, so we'll just have to do it in shifts…"

Most of my schoolmates would have thought that was really bad news, but I was glad to hear it. I'd been wondering whether we'd be having lessons. I liked Lady Musgrave a lot, and Hilda was nice too, once you got past the doom and gloom. But I could see I'd soon get bored if I had to stay in the house every day. Besides, I'd always enjoyed going to school, hard as that might be to believe! Although how long we'd be staying in Devon and going to school here seemed to be anybody's guess.

The rest of Sunday passed slowly after Miss Harrison went. The best part was helping Hilda bake a cake, but that was soon over. Lady Musgrave asked if I wanted to do some gardening with her. That might have been fun, but I was too busy keeping an eye out for Smoky to enjoy it. I didn't want Lady Musgrave to see him, and luckily he didn't appear.

He did come back to my room later, and he ate the food I'd sneaked up for him. But he was gone again in the morning. At breakfast, Arthur came up to the house to speak to Lady Musgrave. He didn't look happy.

"Lost another couple of chicks last night, your Ladyship," he muttered. "Not sure it's a fox, either. Found some fur on the wire, but it were black."

Black fur? My blood froze as a terrible thought occurred to me.

What if it was Smoky who was taking Arthur's chicks?

CHAPTER TWELVE

After breakfast, Lady Musgrave said Arthur would drive me to the village in her car. I should have been excited at the prospect, I suppose. I mean, if anybody had told me a few days before that I'd be on my way to school in a chauffeur-driven car I'd have thought they were barmy.

But I was far too worried to enjoy the ride. I didn't want to spend the day away from Lady Musgrave's house. If I was right about Smoky, then he was in terrible danger. Arthur might be waiting for him with his gun next time Smoky decided he fancied a nice meal of young chick. I hated the idea of what that gun might do to my lovely cat. I hated even more the idea that it would be my fault.

After all, Smoky was only doing what came naturally. I was the one who had smuggled him to the country. But what if I'd been right about Mum and Dad? Maybe they had been planning to do what the government wanted. To be honest, I didn't know what to think any more. Dreadful thoughts filled my mind – Mr Hitler, bombs, Arthur's gun, Mum and Dad and Smoky getting hurt – and I groaned.

"You all right in the back there?" said Arthur, glancing over his shoulder.

"Er… I'm fine," I squeaked. I wasn't, but then what else could I say? Please don't shoot my cat, Arthur – he's nice really, even if he IS eating your chicks…

The funny thing is that I almost did say it. I couldn't get the words out, though. Arthur dropped me off in the village and I watched him drive away. He was coming to collect me later, but not till four o'clock – Miss Harrison had said they were going to try and make it a normal school day. But how could it be normal? I'd be doing my lessons while Arthur probably went hunting for Smoky with his gun…

It was chaos in the church hall. Only about half the kids actually turned up, and most were late. There were no blackboards or desks, so we had to sit on the floor, and we didn't have any books to work from, or exercise books or pencils to write with. The classes were all mixed up, lots of the kids were badly behaved, and the teachers didn't seem able to cope. Mr Jenner got more and more grumpy.

We did our times tables for a while, everyone saying them together. We did some singing too – Miss Harrison played the old out-of-tune piano that stood at one end of the hall. Usually I like singing, especially with Miss Harrison, but I barely opened my mouth. I sat in a corner behind everyone else, keeping my head down, worrying myself sick about Smoky, desperately trying to work out what I should do.

I could keep him shut up in my room, I thought, so long as he made it through today, that is. But I realized that was a stupid plan. Smoky would hate being shut indoors and he'd probably make so much noise Hilda or Lady Musgrave would hear him. I thought briefly of running away with Smoky – but where would we go? He might be able to survive in the country, but I wasn't sure I could.

No, it was beginning to look as if there was only one thing I could do. I would have to confess and beg for mercy – a bit for me, and a lot more for Smoky. And there was only one person I could confess to – Miss Harrison.

I waited until dinner time. Those snooty-looking ladies from our first night turned up with more sandwiches and cake and squash, and said they'd brought us 'lunch'. Everyone piled in, of course, just like before. Once we'd eaten – it all vanished even more quickly this time – Mr Jenner said we could go and play in the churchyard. But I hung back – I wanted to speak to Miss Harrison when nobody else was around.

"Could I have a word, Miss?" I said eventually. "I need to tell you something."

"Of course you can, Betty!" she said, looking concerned. "I'm here to help."

I'd decided I was going to keep it short, be honest, and stay calm. So I took a deep breath, opened my mouth – and burst into tears. I howled and sobbed, and then the whole story came pouring out. A lot of other stuff came pouring out with it, all my worries about Mum and Dad and the war and them getting bombed. I stopped in the end, and Miss Harrison – the wonderful Miss Harrison – gave me a hug.

"Oh, Betty," she said, shaking her head, but with a smile. "You brought your cat all the way from London? In that suitcase of yours? I'm amazed he's still alive!"

"He might not be soon," I said. "I'm worried that Arthur... that he'll..."

"Well, let's make sure that Arthur doesn't, all right?" said Miss Harrison.

I nodded, and blew my nose in Miss Harrison's lacy handkerchief. She went off to talk to Mr Jenner, who frowned and spluttered, and then the two snooty-looking ladies joined in the conversation. They all kept turning to look at me, so the kids in the hall quickly realized something was going on and all sorts of whispering and pointing began. I took no notice, and eventually Miss Harrison came back.

"We're in luck, Betty!" she said. "We're getting a lift to Lady Musgrave's!"

I only hoped we would get there in time.

CHAPTER THIRTEEN

It was one of the snooty-looking ladies who gave us a lift, but it turned out she wasn't quite as snooty as I'd thought. In fact she seemed very nice, and she drove us back to the house as quickly as she could. It still wasn't quick enough for me, though. The journey seemed to take ages. At one point we even got stuck behind a horse-drawn cart full of hay. It blocked the road, but we managed to get round it at last.

Hilda let us in and went to fetch Lady Musgrave from the garden. "This is rather a surprise, Betty," said Lady Musgrave when she came in. "Is something wrong?"

"We have to save Smoky!" I wailed before Miss Harrison could speak. Then I burst into tears for the second time that day. It was daft, but I couldn't help myself.

Miss Harrison explained everything, and I have to say Lady Musgrave took it all pretty well. I'd been expecting her to tell Miss Harrison to take me away and never bring me back, but she didn't. She actually smiled instead. "Well, Betty, you clearly have hidden depths," she said. "And don't worry, I'm sure we can sort this out. Hilda, would you please go and tell Arthur that I'd like to have a word with him?"

Arthur listened to Lady Musgrave and didn't seem very impressed. "A cat, you say?" he muttered with a scowl. "Well, I don't care what it is. If the bloomin' creature is after my chicks, then it's fair game. If I catch it round my coop, I'll…"

"You won't do anything, Arthur," snapped Hilda. "Can't you see how upset the poor child is?" She pointed at me just as I blew my nose into Miss Harrison's lacy hanky. "Anyway, that ancient gun of yours would probably blow up if you fired it!"

"But what about my chicks?" said Arthur.

"I reckon I've lost half a dozen."

"There's no point in crying over spilt milk now, is there, Arthur?" said Lady Musgrave. "I'm certain Betty will keep an eye on her cat from now on."

"Oh, I promise I will! I'll make sure he doesn't get up to any more mischief!" I didn't know if I'd be able to, but it seemed the right thing to say.

"Good, that's all settled," said Lady Musgrave. "You can relax, Betty."

After that, Lady Musgrave asked Hilda to make some tea. Hilda served it to us with cake in the room with the wireless, although Lady Musgrave didn't turn it on. Apparently the news was worse than ever, with more bombing in Poland. After a while the lady who had driven us from the village said she had to go. But Miss Harrison said she could stay longer.

Pretty soon she and Lady Musgrave were getting along like a house on fire. Lady Musgrave asked lots of questions about the evacuation, and how it had all gone.

"Getting the children here was the easy part," said Miss Harrison. "Keeping up their schooling is going to be a lot more difficult. The church hall is just too small."

Suddenly I had a brainwave. "There's plenty of room here," I said. "I bet you could fit everyone in, Florence, and you did say you wanted to feel more… useful…"

I was slowing down because they were giving me strange looks. Miss Harrison seemed a bit shocked, but Lady Musgrave's expression was more thoughtful.

"Why, Betty!" said Miss Harrison. "You shouldn't use Lady Musgrave's Christian name. It's not really your place to make that kind of suggestion, either."

"It's perfectly all right, I told Betty she could call me Florence," said Lady Musgrave, smiling at me. "And actually, I rather like her suggestion…"

Then Lady Musgrave and Miss Harrison talked for what felt like ages. Later, Arthur drove Miss Harrison back to the village, and I went searching for Smoky. It didn't take long to find him in the garden – he came as soon as I called, and I took him into the kitchen. Hilda had a bowl of scraps ready and waiting.

"Look at that!" she said as he licked the bowl clean. "Your cat likes his food almost as much as you. So you can be miserable together when they start rationing."

Smoky was soon treating Lady Musgrave's house like it was his second home. He strolled round the rooms, examining everything and having a good sniff. Then he curled up for a sleep on the settee next to Lady Musgrave herself. I went to shoo him off – Mum doesn't like him to sit on the furniture, and I thought Lady Musgrave might feel the same. But she stroked him till he was purring loudly.

"Don't worry, Betty," she said. "I like cats. We used to have one when the children were small, and I know how fond they were of him. I'm sure they would have been very cross with me if I'd agreed to have him put down for no reason. But I would never have done that, and I have a feeling your parents wouldn't either…"

We looked at each other, and I could feel myself blushing. I'd told Miss Harrison and Lady Musgrave everything. So they knew I hadn't written to Mum and Dad because I'd been cross with them. I wasn't cross now, about Smoky or even being sent away. Mum and Dad had only been trying to protect me, just like I'd been trying to protect Smoky. Lady Musgrave – Florence – was probably right, anyway.

None of it mattered any more. The truth was that I missed my Mum and Dad.

So that night, before I went to bed, I wrote them a long letter. I thought I'd better own up in it to everything I'd done. '*Dear Mum and Dad, how are you? I'm fine. You might have been wondering where Smoky has been over the last few days…*'

CHAPTER FOURTEEN

I got away with it, thank goodness. Mum wrote me a long letter back, and she was so pleased to hear from me she forgot to tell me off. She did say they'd wondered where Smoky had got to. I'd explained in my letter why I'd taken him with me, and Mum had said they knew other people were having their pets put down. But she'd also said they would never have done such a thing. They knew how much I loved him.

So everything was fine. Now all I had to do was get used to being evacuated, and that should have been dead easy. I had my own room, an inside toilet, loads of lovely grub.

I liked Lady Musgrave and Hilda, and even Arthur stopped being so grumpy once he'd sorted out the wire on the chicken coop and made it a lot stronger. I caught him giving Smoky the evil eye every so often, but Smoky wasn't bothered.

Things soon got quite lively at Lady Musgrave's house too. She loved my idea about using part of the house as a school for evacuated kids, and it was up and running before the end of the week. Some of the empty rooms were turned into classrooms, and Lady Musgrave even organized a coach to bring the kids in every day. Mr Jenner and Miss Harrison were so grateful, and soon the lessons were almost like normal.

But all I wanted was to go home. I wrote to Mum and Dad a lot over the next few weeks, and every time I got a letter back from them I felt more homesick. I wasn't the only one. Most of the kids felt the same, although some said they didn't miss their parents. But then I suppose not everyone gets on with their parents, and maybe the people who'd taken those kids in were nicer, and had nicer houses.

After a month or so I was dead miserable. But luckily, Mr Hitler came to my rescue. He wasn't doing much. He had conquered Poland by the end of September, and after that things went very quiet. Mr Hitler certainly didn't send his planes to bomb London, or anywhere else in Britain, either. So a lot of parents said the evacuation had been a waste of time, and wanted their kids back.

Mr Jenner resisted for a while, but by the end of October he'd given up. More than half the kids went home, and I was one of them. There wouldn't be a special train for us this time, though. We had to travel on an ordinary train, like anybody else.

On the day, Lady Musgrave wanted to see me off at the station, so Arthur drove us there. I had a couple of goodbyes to say before I could leave. I was desperate to go home, but I knew I was going to miss Lady Musgrave, and Hilda and Arthur too.

The first goodbye was to Hilda. She'd made me a huge packed lunch. "You're making a big mistake," she said. "I wouldn't go to that London if you paid me…"

The second was to Smoky! I'd decided he'd be better off in the country, and Lady Musgrave said she'd be happy for him to stay. He had his own bed now, an old basket Hilda had found for him and put in the corner of the kitchen. I knelt and stroked him and tried not to blub. "Behave yourself, Smoky," I whispered into his straight ear, and he purred. "I'll come back and get you when this stupid war is over."

I did cry once we were in the car, and Lady Musgrave gave me a hug. Arthur was looking at us in the rear-view mirror, and I swear there was a tear in his eye too.

"Don't worry, Betty," said Lady Musgrave. "Smoky will be fine with us. I'll write and tell you how he's getting on. And I expect you to write back to me."

Miss Harrison was on the train to look after us kids, and we both waved to Lady Musgrave and Arthur as it pulled out. I could hardly believe I was going home.

But that isn't the end of the story. Things stayed quiet for the next few months, and people even started to say the war wasn't real – Mr Hitler wasn't attacking us and we weren't attacking him. The papers called it 'The Phoney War.' Mr Hitler was being dead crafty, though – as we found out, he was waiting till we let our guard down. Suddenly, in the spring of the next year – 1940 – he threw everything at us.

Mum and I listened to the news on the wireless every night, and it was awful. Denmark and Norway quickly fell to the Germans, then Holland and Belgium and France. It was just Mum and me because

Dad had volunteered as a soldier.

He'd joined up in time to go and fight in France, but the Germans were unstoppable. They beat us and the French. Our soldiers were surrounded at a French port called Dunkirk, and had to be rescued by the Navy and lots of little boats manned by volunteers. Dad was all right – he was on one of the last boats out, and he stayed with his regiment, guarding the south coast. Now Britain stood alone. Mr Chamberlain stepped down, and we got a new Prime Minister, Mr Churchill.

But we didn't give in, not even when the terrible bombing really did start.

It happened a year after I'd been evacuated – now the war wasn't phoney any more. Mr Hitler sent his planes to London every night, and it was bad. Mum and I soon got used to sleeping in the air raid shelter at the end of our road. Bombs fell, houses were blown up and lots of people were killed. Mr Hitler was unleashing his 'blitzkrieg' on us, which is the German for 'lightning' war. We just shortened it to Blitz. It seemed like exactly the right word for what we were going through.

One night it looked like everywhere north of the river was burning. "Right, that's it," said Mum the next morning. A house in our street had been hit too, and a whole family had been killed – including a couple of young kids. "I'm sending you back to that posh lady in the country. I should never have let you come home…"

I'd been expecting this. Loads of the kids who'd been evacuated and returned were being packed off again. I knew Mum only wanted what was best for me, and it would definitely be safer in Devon. Part of me liked the idea of seeing Smoky again, and Lady Musgrave and Hilda and even Arthur. I also knew Lady Musgrave would have me back there like a shot. But another part of me felt completely different.

I'd never wanted to be evacuated in the first place, and I didn't want to go now.

With Dad away fighting, I couldn't leave Mum by herself. Not when she was really in danger – even though it meant I'd be in danger too.

"Leave off, Mum," I said. "I don't care what you say, I'm not going."

Mum argued with me, of course, and for a while I thought she wasn't going to give up – Dad says she can be as stubborn as me, sometimes. But she did in the end.

"Oh well," she said with a deep sigh. "You can't blame me for trying."

"Don't worry, Mum," I said. "We'll just have to stick it out together."

And amazingly enough – we did.

EPILOGUE

Betty was one of hundreds of thousands of children who were evacuated from the cities of Britain to the countryside in the first few days of the Second World War. Over 800,000 children were evacuated in the first four days of September 1939, along with 100,000 adults to look after them – teachers, mostly, but some parents as well. Half a million mothers were evacuated with their pre-school children too.

Betty's experience wasn't unusual. The evacuation went smoothly in some areas, but there were plenty of problems. In the 'reception areas', the local people were often expecting far fewer children than actually turned up. Finding homes for them was difficult, and there were no schools for them to go to either. Many of the schools in the cities were also closed because the teachers had been evacuated.

The government had planned the evacuation because they really believed the cities would be heavily bombed. They thought up to four million people would be killed immediately. As Betty and the rest of the country discovered, this didn't happen – there was almost no bombing in the early months of the war. That's why over half of the evacuated children returned to their homes in the cities by Christmas 1939.

Then, in the summer and autumn of 1940, France fell and the German air-force did start bombing British cities. Many of the children who had returned were evacuated once more to escape the air raids of the Blitz – although like Betty, quite a few stayed behind with their families. There were more evacuations later in the war, particularly in 1944 when Hitler attacked Britain with his deadly 'flying bombs' and rockets.

By the end of the war, over three million people had been evacuated at one time or another. Like Betty, some children from very ordinary homes found themselves living with rich families who did things very differently. Many children loved their 'new' families – others didn't get on so well with them, and of course there was a lot of homesickness. The whole experience certainly changed many people forever.